Santa Claus
is Coming
to Town

Written by SARAH ERSKINE

Illustrated by NIGEL McMULLEN

Derrydale Books

New York/Avenel, New Jersey

A TEMPLAR BOOK

This 1992 edition published by Derrydale Books,
distributed by Outlet Book Company, Inc., a Random House Company,
40 Engelhard Avenue, Avenel, New Jersey 07001.

First published in Canada in 1992 by Smithbooks,
113 Merton Street, Toronto, Canada M45 1AB.

Devised and produced by The Templar Company plc,
Pippbrook Mill, London Road, Dorking, Surrey RH4 1JE, Great Britain.

Edited by A J Wood
Designed by Janie Louise Hunt
Printed and bound in Singapore

ISBN 0-517-06970-9
8 7 6 5 4 3 2 1

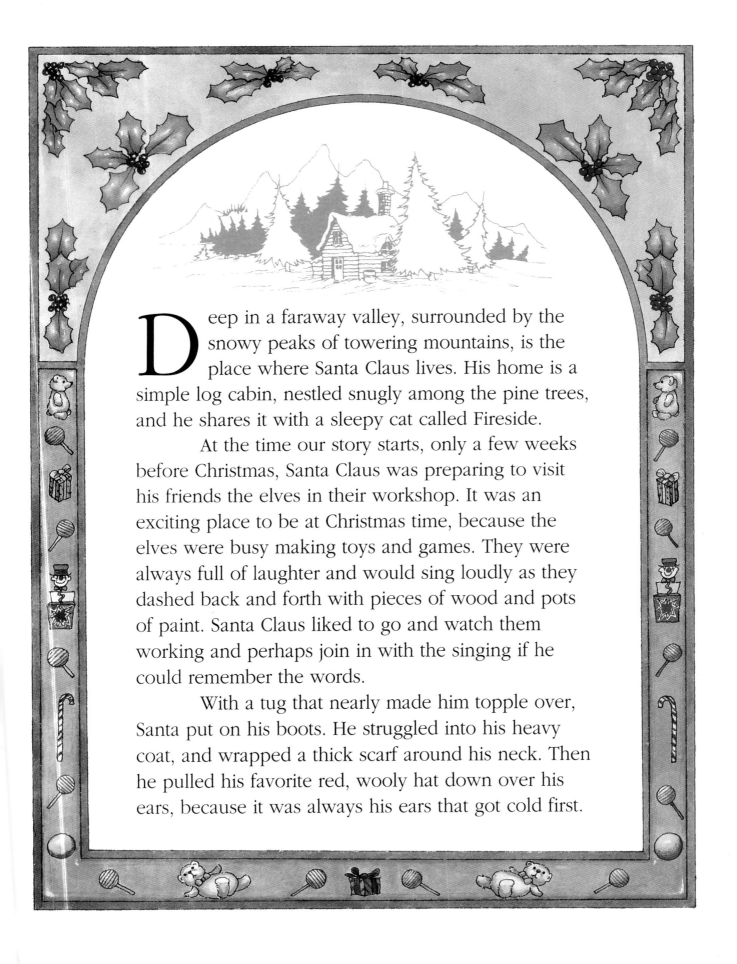

Deep in a faraway valley, surrounded by the snowy peaks of towering mountains, is the place where Santa Claus lives. His home is a simple log cabin, nestled snugly among the pine trees, and he shares it with a sleepy cat called Fireside.

At the time our story starts, only a few weeks before Christmas, Santa Claus was preparing to visit his friends the elves in their workshop. It was an exciting place to be at Christmas time, because the elves were busy making toys and games. They were always full of laughter and would sing loudly as they dashed back and forth with pieces of wood and pots of paint. Santa Claus liked to go and watch them working and perhaps join in with the singing if he could remember the words.

With a tug that nearly made him topple over, Santa put on his boots. He struggled into his heavy coat, and wrapped a thick scarf around his neck. Then he pulled his favorite red, wooly hat down over his ears, because it was always his ears that got cold first.

Santa stepped out into the white, crunchy snow, took a deep breath of fresh, mountain air, and began the walk to the workshop. He followed a narrow, winding path between the pine trees and saw the rays of sunlight make the snow glisten. He trod carefully over a small bridge and looked down to see the icy blue water as it tinkled over smooth pebbles. As he walked, he hummed a happy tune and thought about Christmas Eve, for it was the most exciting time of the year for Santa Claus. It was the night of *The Great Delivery of Presents* to all the children who had been good and well-behaved.

In the distance, Santa could see the workshop but he could not hear the elves singing or laughing.

"Perhaps the wind is carrying the sound away," he thought, and he carried on happily humming. But as he drew closer, he *could* hear the elves – instead of laughter, he heard angry shouting!

Santa quickened his pace and threw open the door of the workshop. Inside, a sorry scene met his eyes. Two of the elves, Bright and Chuckles, were standing in the middle of the room, both clutching the same comic book and refusing to give it up.

"Let go of my book!" shouted Chuckles.

"It's not yours!" yelled Bright. "It's mine!"

"Bright! Chuckles!" cried Santa. "Whatever is the matter? Why are you arguing like this?"

"Chuckles took my book," howled Bright.

"I did not!" bellowed Chuckles, angrily.

"But can't you share your things like you usually do?" Santa asked them.

"No!!!" shrieked both the elves at once, and they pulled the book so hard that it ripped right down the middle.

"Now see what has happened," sighed Santa. "Because you were both being selfish, you have spoiled the book for everyone."

"I don't care," pouted Chuckles.

"It was a stupid book anyway," said Bright.

Santa looked unhappily at the workshop. It was usually clean and tidy, but toys and books had been thrown everywhere and he could even see an old sandwich that had been squashed into the carpet. Some of the elves still lounged half-asleep in their beds, while others sat throwing things at each other and being rude. Santa could also see that they had not made any toys or gifts for *The Great Delivery of Presents*.

"Why are you behaving like this?" asked Santa. "The children are going to be so disappointed if there are no presents for them."

The biggest elf, whose name was Sprite, looked up at Santa with a frown.

"We don't care about the children," he said. "None of the children does as he or she is told, so we don't see why *we* should."

"Oh, dear me!" sighed Santa, and he shook his head sadly. "I know that there are some bad children in the world, but most of them are good. So if *you* are being too naughty to make any toys, then I shall jolly well make them myself! Now I had better go and see how the reindeer are getting on. They will be very sad to hear how naughty you are being."

Santa turned and slowly left the workshop.
Behind him he could hear the raised voices of the
elves as they began quarreling and squabbling again.

The wind was cold. It tugged at Santa's clothes
as he trudged through the snow to the stables where
the reindeer lived. Snow flakes settled on his beard,
and instead of looking at the beautiful scenery around
him, he stared gloomily at his boots.

Inside the stables it was warm and cozy.
Lanterns hung from the ceiling and gave out a golden

glow. But Santa looked about and was dismayed to see that all the harnesses, which hung upon the walls, were dirty and unpolished. The silver bells that were used to decorate the sleigh were tarnished and dull instead of bright and shiny. Even the sleigh itself sat in a dark and dusty corner, covered in cobwebs and bits of straw. It was obvious that the reindeer had done nothing in preparation for *The Great Delivery of Presents*. In fact, they were all sitting or standing in front of the fire doing nothing at all.

"Why aren't you getting ready for Christmas?" Santa asked them anxiously.

One of the reindeer looked sadly at Santa.

"There isn't going to be a delivery this year, Santa," he moaned.

"Don't be silly," laughed Santa. "I shall make some toys myself and we can still do the delivery."

"Haven't you read the news?" the reindeer grunted, and nodded his head toward a newspaper. Santa picked it up and read the front page. In big black letters the headline read,

NEWS

CHILDREN TOO BAD FOR CHRISTMAS PRESENTS

Santa gasped. The report said that children everywhere were being rude, grumpy, disobedient, selfish, and unkind. Santa could hardly believe it. He slumped into a chair and put his head in his hands.

He could only deliver presents to children who were good. If there were no good children, Santa would be out of a job, and he didn't know how to do anything else. He had once tried to be a plumber, but he caused so many floods that he had to give it up.

Santa sat and thought, shaking his head sadly every now and then. Suddenly he jumped up.

"I'm not going to believe what it says in the newspapers!" he cried. "I think that there must be some good, kind children in the world."

"You're wasting your time, Santa," sighed another reindeer. "I bet you won't be able to find a single good child anywhere."

"Well, I think I can," said Santa. "It's my job, after all." And he left the stables and crunched back through the snow to his cabin.

Going straight to one of the shelves, he took down a huge roll of paper called *The Great Map of Everywhere*. It was too big to fit on the table, so he spread it out over the floor. Then he held a pin high above his head, and made big circles in the air with it.

Closing his eyes tight, Santa stuck the pin into the map. He opened his eyes to see where it had landed because, wherever it was, that would be the place where he would begin his search for the one good child. He looked down at *The Great Map of Everywhere* and …

"Oh dear me!" chortled Santa. "The pin has landed in the sea. There won't be any children there. I'll have to try again."

So again Santa closed his eyes, waved the pin in the air and stuck it into the map. This time it had landed in a place called Greenville.

"Then Greenville is where I shall go!" announced Santa loudly, making Fireside jump in surprise. Wasting no time, Santa wrapped an extra scarf around his neck, pulled his hat down over his ears again, and said goodbye to Fireside.

Outside the cabin, Santa tipped back his head and looked at the sky. It was late in the afternoon and beginning to get dark.

"Excuse me!" he called up to a cloud. "Are you going anywhere near Greenville!"

"Why yes," the cloud called back. "I'm on my way there now to deliver some snow. I can take you there, if you like." And the cloud lowered itself down to the ground, sprinkling a flurry of white snowflakes as it came. Santa climbed aboard and the cloud sailed

up and away. They were soon high over the trees and mountains. The stars winked in the dark night sky and, looking down, Santa could see the tiny, twinkling dots of light from the towns and cities below. Santa snuggled deep into the fluffy cloud and soon fell fast asleep. He dreamed of hot chocolate pudding and of trees that grew toffees.

When Santa awoke it was morning, and the cloud had already sprinkled a thick layer of snow over Greenville Town. Stretching and yawning, Santa thanked the cloud for a lovely journey and waved goodbye as it sailed back into the sky. Then he stood and looked around.

Greenville was a small town with some shops, a park and playground, and streets of snug, snow-covered houses. Santa took a notebook and a short, stubby pencil out of his pocket, and set off to find

some nice children so that he could make a list of
their names. As he walked, his ears began to feel very
cold, and putting his hand up to his head he realized
that his hat had gone.

"Oh dear me!" he tutted. "I must have dropped
it somewhere." So Santa began to retrace his footsteps
through the snow looking all around for his wooly hat.

Suddenly he heard someone crying. He looked
up and saw a girl leaning out of her bedroom window.
Her face was angry and red with rage.

"Whatever is the matter?" Santa called up to
her. The girl looked down and when she saw Santa
she scowled. She did not recognize him without his
red, wooly hat.

"I'm not allowed out to play!" she wailed.

"Why not?" asked Santa.

"Because I made a mess of my bedroom and threw my toys everywhere!" she sobbed.

"Oh well," laughed Santa. "I'm sure you'll be able to play if you tidy your room quickly."

"But I don't want to!" she shouted rudely, and she slammed the window shut!

"Goodness me!" said Santa. "I don't think that little girl can go on my list." And he carried on walking down the street.

As he was passing a garden he saw a boy kicking a garbage can furiously. When Santa asked him what the matter was he carried on kicking and spoke in a loud, grumpy voice.

"I've got to look after my kid sister because my mom's not well and it means I can't play baseball with the other boys."

"But surely you don't mind if your mother's not well?" Santa was very surprised.

"Kid sisters aren't any fun and it's not fair!" the boy complained.

Santa walked on and on, but he could not find his red, wooly hat or any nice children. They were, as the newspaper had said, rude and bad-tempered. His ears were getting colder and colder, so he went into a shop to buy a new hat, but they had completely sold out of red, wooly ones. As Santa left the shop he noticed a big sign outside the Santa's Toyshop. It read,

CLOSED
NO
SANTA
THIS YEAR

Santa walked around the playground and then around the park and after a while he sat down on a bench. His ears were very cold, and he rubbed them with his hands to try and warm them. He looked at his notebook, but there were still no names in it. Feeling very cold, hungry, and miserable, Santa decided that the reindeer must have been right. There was not a single good child left.

"I shall have to go home," he thought
unhappily, "and start looking for another job." And he
rubbed his ears again in an effort to warm them up.

"Excuse me," said a small voice by his side,
"but are your ears cold?"

"Yes, they are," said Santa, looking round to
see a small boy standing beside him. "Have you seen
a red, wooly hat anywhere?"

"No," replied the little boy. "But you can have
mine." And promptly he took off his hat and handed it
to Santa. Santa tried putting it on, but it was too small.

"My Dad has a hat that he never wears," said the little boy. "Why don't you come to my house for tea and we'll ask if you can borrow it. We're going to have hot chocolate pudding and custard, and mom said that I could bring a friend home if I wanted."

"Chocolate pudding! Why that would be lovely!" cried Santa and his eyes twinkled happily. At last he had found a child who was good and kind-hearted. "I must put you on my list," he said excitedly, introducing himself. The boy said that his name was

Evan, and that he was very pleased to meet the real Santa Claus. Then they shook hands and began walking through the snow.

When they arrived at Evan's home, Santa shook hands with Evan's father and gave a deep bow to his mother, and they told Santa that any friend of Evan's was a friend of theirs. They all sat around the fire and Santa's ears got warmer and warmer as he ate the hot chocolate pudding. Soon Santa had told them all about the elves and the reindeer, and how difficult it was to find any nice children.

"Why don't you take Evan to the workshop to prove that not all children are horrible?" suggested Evan's father. Evan smiled a huge smile.

"Would you like that?" asked Santa.

"I'd love to!" said Evan, and he became so excited that he could hardly sit still. Evan's mother agreed that he could go, and while she made them a flask of hot coffee for the journey, Santa went outside

to call another cloud. He looked up, and there was the same snowcloud that had given him a ride the night before.

"I've been looking for you," called the cloud. "You left your hat behind." And sure enough, when Evan and Santa climbed on to the cloud, there was the red, wooly hat. Santa quickly pulled it right down over his ears and the two of them laughed about it for the whole journey.

When Santa and Evan arrived in the faraway valley, they went straight to the elves' workshop.

It was even more untidy now and the elves were still fighting and arguing with each other. Evan looked at them all and then he said in a very loud voice:

"Is it fun being so naughty?"

Suddenly, the workshop went very quiet. The elves stopped what they were doing and looked at Evan in stunned silence.

"Of course it's fun!" snapped Bright, angrily. "We don't have to do what we're told, we can make a

mess, we can even stay up all night if we want to. We can all do exactly what we want." Bright scowled at the other elves to make sure that they agreed. Then, in the quiet, there suddenly came the sound of sobbing. It was coming from the top of one of the bunk beds.

"I... I... I don't think it's fun," said a small, wobbly voice, and the pink, tear-stained face of Tot, the smallest elf, appeared from underneath the bedclothes.

"We don't play nice games anymore, because nobody plays fair," he gulped. "And I miss making toys for all the children. And the reindeer aren't friends with us. And Santa doesn't like us any more. And I don't want to stay up all night because I get too tired. And nobody laughs … and … and nobody hugs me any more." With that, poor little Tot burst into tears again and burrowed his face into his pillow. And then, one by one, all the other elves burst into tears as well.

"We're sorry, Tot," wailed Chuckles. "We didn't mean to make you unhappy. And you're right, being bad isn't that much fun after all."

All the elves gave Tot a hug. And then they hugged Santa, and then Evan, and then they hugged each other and Chuckles even tried hugging himself, but he fell over and started laughing. Soon, all the other elves were laughing too and they began straight away to tidy the workshop.

"We want to make lots of lovely presents for Christmas now," said Chuckles, "but who will you give them to, Santa? Evan is the only nice child you managed to find."

"Don't you worry. There must be lots of other good children," laughed Santa. "I shall find them." So Chuckles ran to tell the reindeer that Christmas was going ahead as usual and everyone began working furiously to get ready for *The Great Delivery of Presents*.

Evan caught a fast cloud back to Greenville
and told all his friends about Tot and the other elves.
The children felt guilty about having been so badly
behaved and they also realized that it was more fun to
be good because people liked them more. Gradually
the news spread and children everywhere started
being good and kind and feeling a lot better for it.

Santa flew over the towns and cities, and soon he had enough names to fill a hundred notebooks.

Meanwhile, the reindeer cleaned and scrubbed and brushed. The sleigh was given a new coat of paint and they polished the harnesses until they shone. The silver bells sparkled like diamonds and tinkled a merry tune.

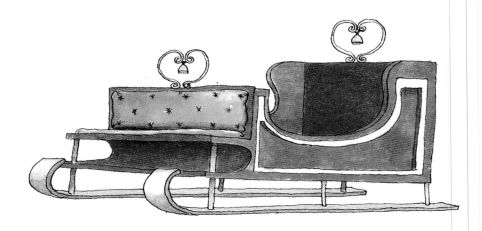

In the workshop, the elves were busy sawing, hammering, painting, and wrapping. In one corner there was a pile of presents that grew bigger and bigger with each passing hour. Every one of them worked as hard as they could, and by Christmas Eve everything was ready. The elves gathered outside to wave and cheer the sleigh goodbye as Santa left to start *The Great Delivery.*

The reindeer pranced and danced through the sky, pulling Santa and all the presents behind them. And at the very back of the sleigh was an extra special present for a little boy called Evan who had made them all realize that being good and kind was much more fun than being horrid!